*Para mi mamá con cariño*
*—M. E.*

*For Ana and Peter, always in the front line*
*—R. C.*

SIMON & SCHUSTER BOOKS FOR YOUNG READERS
An imprint of Simon & Schuster Children's Publishing Division
1230 Avenue of the Americas, New York, New York 10020
Text © 2021 by Margarita Engle
Illustrations © 2021 by Raúl Colón
SIMON & SCHUSTER BOOKS FOR YOUNG READERS and related marks are trademarks of Simon & Schuster, Inc.
For information about special discounts for bulk purchases, please contact Simon & Schuster Special Sales
at 1-866-506-1949 or business@simonandschuster.com.
The Simon & Schuster Speakers Bureau can bring authors to your live event. For more information or to book an event,
contact the Simon & Schuster Speakers Bureau at 1-866-248-3049 or visit our website at www.simonspeakers.com.
Book design by Laurent Linn
The text for this book was set in Cabrito.
The illustrations for this book were rendered using Prismacolor colored pencils and lithograph crayons on Fabriano Artistico paper.
Manufactured in China
0921 SCP
First Edition
2  4  6  8  10  9  7  5  3  1
Library of Congress Cataloging-in-Publication Data
Names: Engle, Margarita, author. | Colón, Raúl, illustrator.
Title: Light for all / Margarita Engle ; illustrated by Raúl Colón.
Description: New York : Simon & Schuster Books for Young Readers, Paula Wiseman Books, [2020] | Audience: Ages 4-8. |
Audience: Grades 2-3.  Summary: Illustrations and easy-to-read text tell of travelers who have left their homelands to bring their talents,
hopes, and determination to a land where Liberty's light shines for all.
Identifiers: LCCN 2019052792 (print) | LCCN 2019052793 (eBook) | ISBN 9781534457270 (hardcover) | ISBN 9781534457287 (eBook)
Subjects: CYAC: Immigrants—Fiction. | Statue of Liberty (New York, N.Y.)—Fiction.
Classification: LCC PZ7.E7158 Lig 2020  (print) | LCC PZ7.E7158  (eBook) |
DDC [E]—dc23
LC record available at https://lccn.loc.gov/2019052792
LC eBook record available at https://lccn.loc.gov/2019052793

# Light for All

MARGARITA ENGLE

ILLUSTRATED BY
RAÚL COLÓN

A Paula Wiseman Book
Simon & Schuster Books for Young Readers
New York London Toronto Sydney New Delhi

From land to land,
brave travelers arrive
with hopes, dreams, skills,
and determination.

The powerful light
of a mighty lamp
shines
for all!

Some of us come to join mothers, fathers, sisters, brothers—each joyful family reunion wondrous.

The towering glow
from a lifted torch
greets all.

From land to land,
survivors arrive
escaping from war,
storms, earthquakes,
hunger. . . .

A radiant flame glows for all.

The promise of jobs
brings talented doctors, scientists,
artists, singers, students, cooks,

and farmers who know
how to plant and harvest
delicious food
for everyone.

We have to struggle to be accepted,
because some people don't understand
the need
for equality.

Freedom to speak, read, write,
and believe as we please

helps us join others who came
for the same reasons
long ago.

Immigrants study to learn a new language
without forgetting words from our first homes,
because knowing more than one way
to communicate
is always helpful
to all.

We still love the lands

where we were born,

and we love this new homeland too, as we enter
the long, bitter story of the US, a history
that began with cruel invasions,
stealing land from Native people,
bringing enslaved captives
all the way from Africa, and
then seizing a huge part
of Mexico . . .

but gentler waves of arrival followed,
with newcomers welcomed, so that now
we're part of the Statue of Liberty's
promise,

as her light leaps, loops,
weaves, and dances, creating
shared hope
for all.

# AUTHOR'S NOTE

While praising the Statue of Liberty, people often refer to the United States as a country of immigrants. That phrase ignores the true experiences of Indigenous and African American communities, who were either here before conquerors and immigrants arrived, or were brought by force, kidnapped, and enslaved.

In *Light for All*, I want to show that everyone deserves equality, despite our ancestors' wide variety of backgrounds. My Cuban mother came to California as an immigrant after marrying my Los Angeles–born father, whose parents were immigrants from the Ukraine. My tío Pepe and abuela Fefa arrived in the US as refugees who were granted asylum. Some of my mother's relatives were able to go directly to Florida, while others spent years waiting in Spain or Venezuela.

When my children were little, tío Pepe took us to see the Statue of Liberty. When my Nepali son-in-law visited New York, he saw it too. For all, it remains a beautiful symbol of freedom and equality, inspiring dreams of feeling welcomed, and of welcoming others.

*—M. E.*

# ILLUSTRATOR'S NOTE

My parents, being from Puerto Rico, already had American citizenship when they came to New York. However, they were regarded as immigrants when they arrived. But the doors were open to them and myself when I was born. The Statue of Liberty stands for those open doors. I had the privilege to illustrate this book because of that. Of course Margarita Engle's words led the way. Yes, immigrants are still arriving, and yes, immigrants are what will keep the future alive for the country. They follow the light the Statue of Liberty casts upon them, but now they have the chance to "Be the Light." All these years the Union has proved that. Keep on shining!

*—R. C.*